Greatness in You!

WRITTEN BY DR. LESLIE GRIFFIN
ILLUSTRATED BY DANIEL MAJAN

WestBow Press books may be ordered through booksellers or by contacting:

WestBow Press
A Division of Thomas Nelson & Zondervan
1663 Liberty Drive
Bloomington, IN 47403
www.westbowpress.com
1 (866) 928-1240

ISBN: 978-1-9736-3724-0 (sc)
ISBN: 978-1-9736-3725-7 (e)

Library of Congress Control Number: 2018909665

Print information available on the last page.

WestBow Press rev. date: 8/20/2018

WESTBOW
PRESS®
A DIVISION OF THOMAS NELSON
& ZONDERVAN

This book is dedicated to
the 21st generation.

I see greatness in you!
I can see it in your style.

I can see it in your walk.
I can see it when you smile.

When you laugh, I hear greatness.
When you speak, I hear it more.

I see greatness on your face
as you stand at the door.

When you run, I see greatness.
I can see it in every stride.

I see confidence, I see pizazz,
I see strength, I see pride.

When you enter the room, I see greatness. I can sense it in the air.

I see determination, I see focus,
I see greatness in your stare.

I see greatness in you
little boy, little girl!

I can see it in every flip,
every kick and every twirl.

ROOM A1

ROOM A

I see greatness in process. I see greatness, I do. I see a young mind made for greatness.

SPELLING BEE COMPETITION

I see greatness in you!

The End!

CPSIA information can be obtained
at www.ICGtesting.com
Printed in the USA
LVHW07s0253170918
590361LV00014B/282/P